MY Christmas ACTIVITY BOOK

By Carolyn Owens
Illustrated by Susan Morris

CONCORDIA PUBLISHING HOUSE • SAINT LOUIS

3558 S. Jefferson Avenue, St. Louis, MO 63118-3968
Manufactured in the United States of America

11 12 13 14 15 16 15 14 13 12

So Joseph also went up from the town of Nazareth in Galilee to Judea, to Bethlehem the town of David, because he belonged to the house and line of David. He went there to register with Mary, who was pledged to be married to him and was expecting a child.
(Luke 2:4–5 NIV)

Complete this picture of Mary and Joseph. Connect the dots to draw some traveling clothes and a donkey for them.

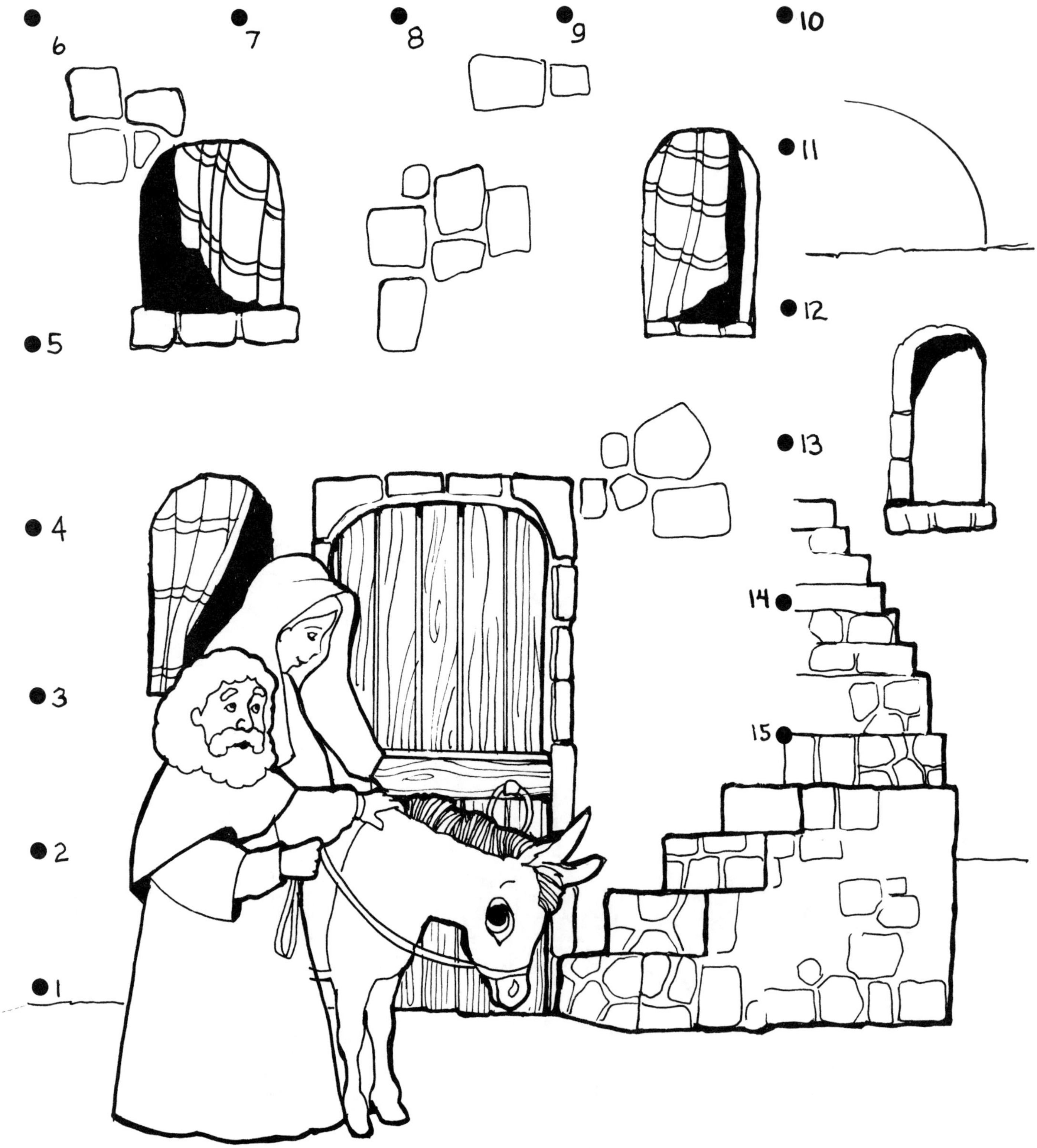

There was no room for them in the inn.

(Luke 2:7 NIV)

Today people stay in hotels or motels when they travel. Complete this building to show what you think an inn in Bethlehem may have looked like when Jesus was born.

While they were there, the time came for the baby to be born, and she gave birth to her firstborn, a son. She wrapped Him in cloths and placed Him in a manger.

(Luke 2:6–7 NIV)

The animals were happy to share their home with baby Jesus. Connect the dots to see who is looking at the manger.

Read Luke 2:1–20 to hear how God sent His Son to be our Savior. If there had been newspapers at the time of Jesus' birth, what would the headline have said? What picture would go with it?

Circle and color the items baby Jesus and Joseph and Mary could have used.

Joseph was a carpenter. Pretend you are a carpenter. Design a special bed for baby Jesus.

How will you finish this birth announcement for baby Jesus?

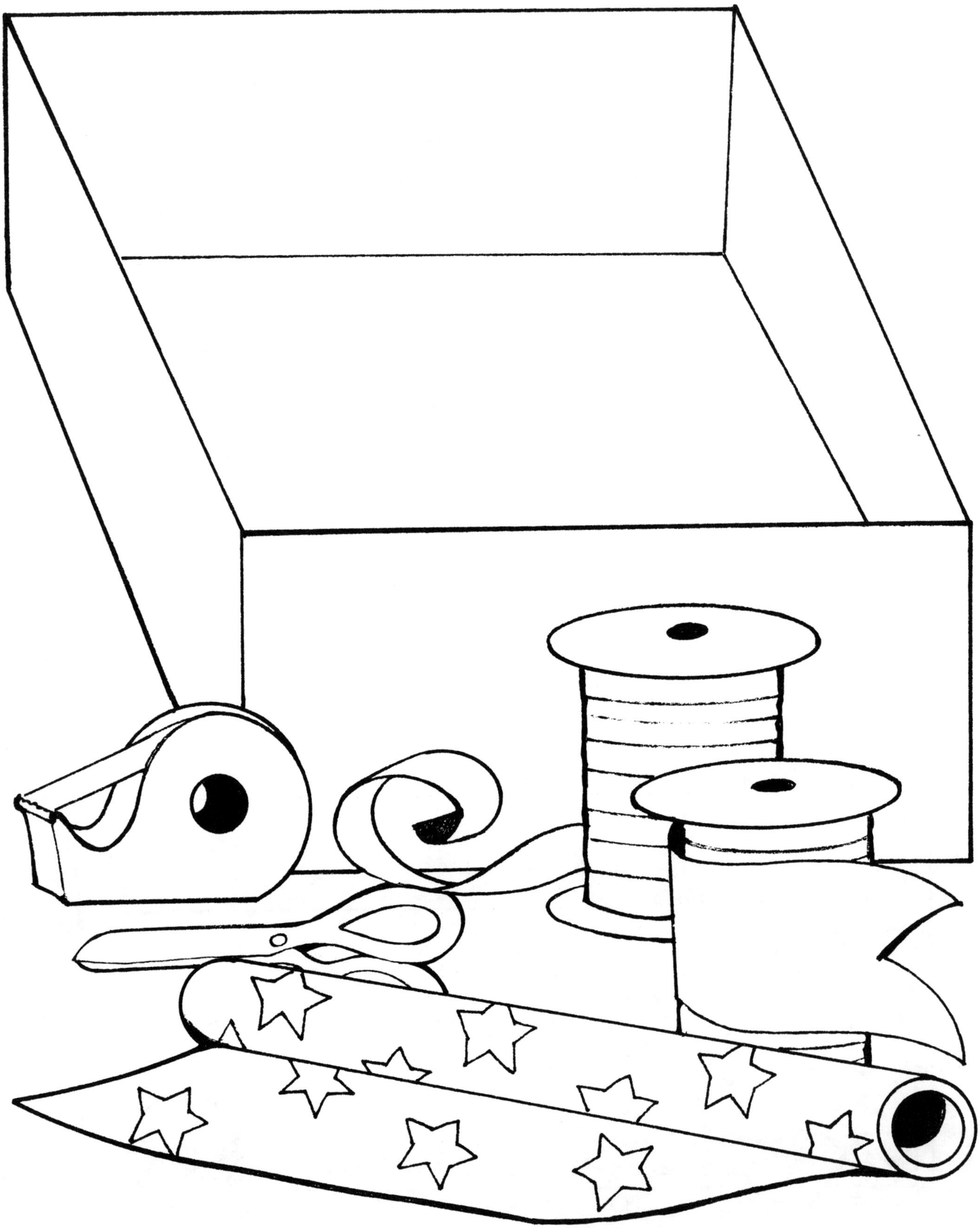

What birthday present would you bring Jesus? Draw a picture or cut a picture from a magazine or catalog and glue it inside this gift box.

Animals, much like the ones which may have been in the stable with Mary, Joseph, and Jesus, are hidden in this picture. Find and color them.

Here is a picture of the Wise Men who saw God's special star in the sky and visited Jesus. They are sometimes called kings. Design a special crown for each one.

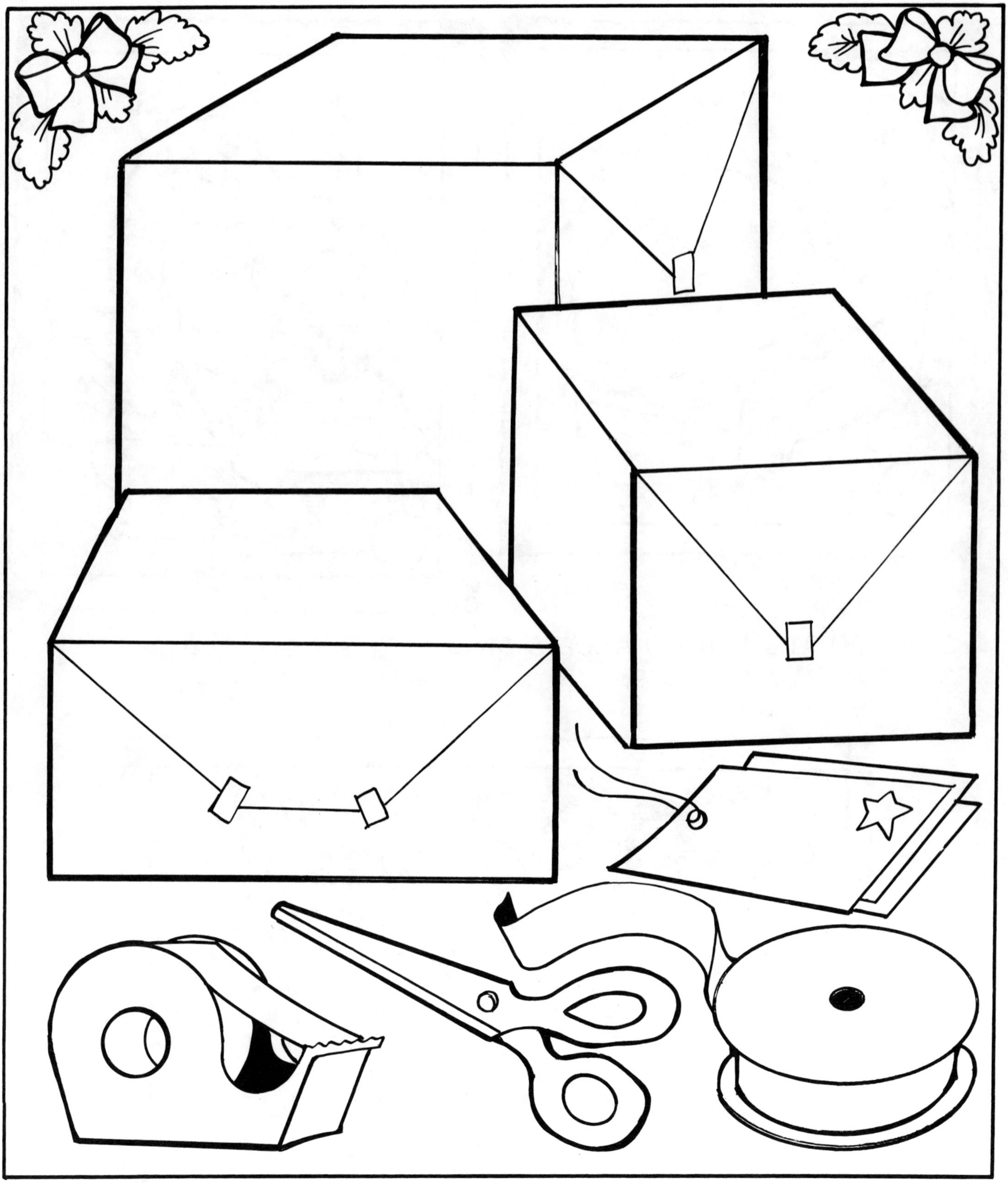

Read Matthew 2:11 in your Bible. The verse mentions three gifts Jesus received. Write the name of each gift on one of the boxes. Then decorate the boxes with gift-wrap and ribbons.

1. WE THREE KINGS
2. HARK! THE HERALD ANGELS SING
3. AWAY IN A MANGER

We sing wonderful songs about Jesus at Christmas time. Draw a line to match each picture to the correct song title. Then color the pictures.

Design a flag to welcome baby Jesus on Christmas Day.

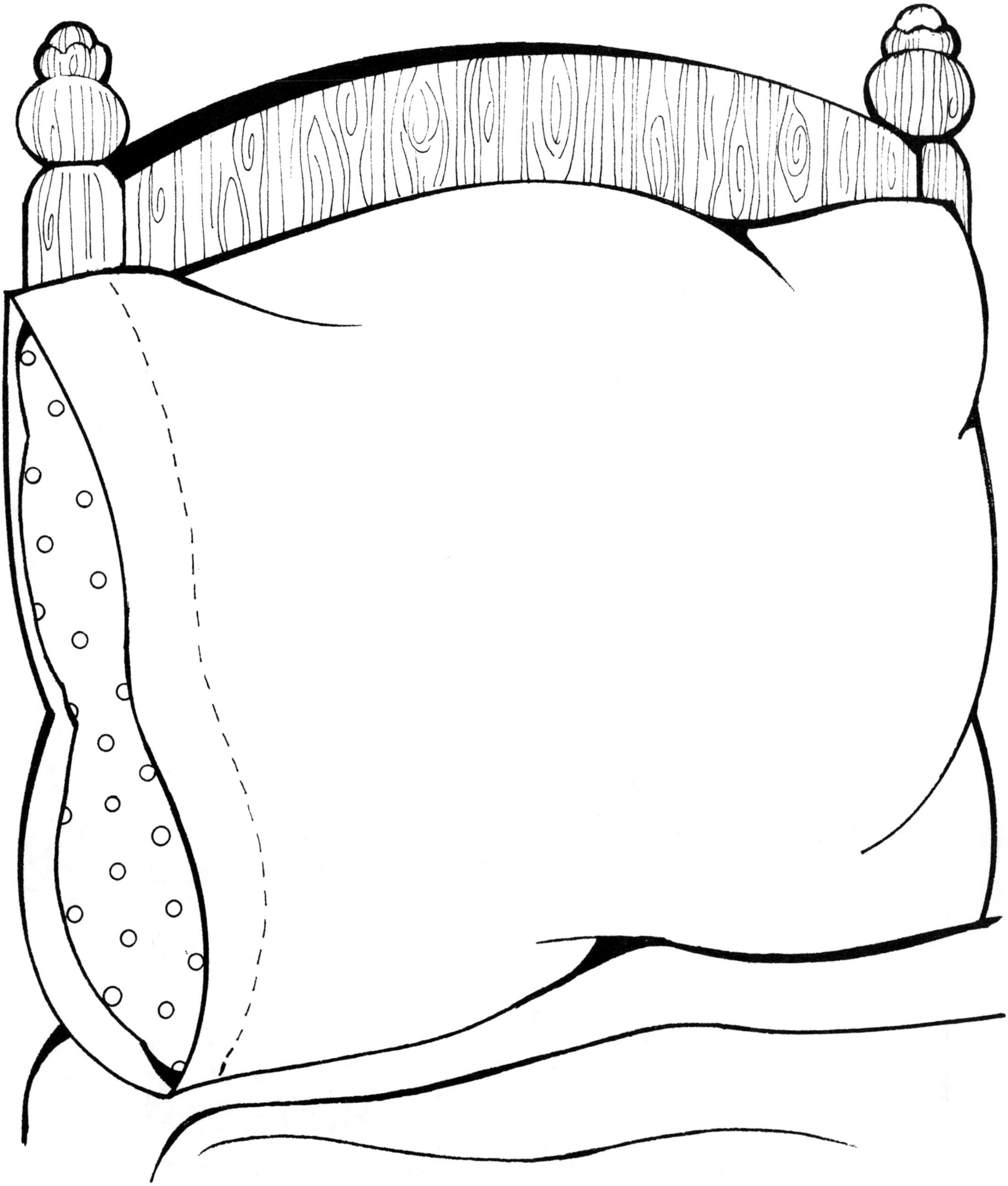

Mary wrapped baby Jesus in soft cloths and laid Him in a bed of hay. Use crayons or markers to decorate this pillow as a special birthday gift for Jesus.

God loves us so much, He sent His only Son Jesus to be born as a baby. When Jesus grew up, He died on the cross to take the punishment for our sins and rose again to win us life with Him. Use this piece of paper to tell Jesus how you feel about His coming to earth to save you.

We sing lots of good songs about Jesus at Christmas. Design this CD jacket to picture your favorite carol about Jesus.

It is fun to eat birthday cake on your birthday. Connect the dots and decorate this cake for Jesus' birthday.

For God so loved the world that He gave His one and only Son, that whoever believes in Him shall not perish but have eternal life.

(John 3:16 NIV)

God sent His one and only Son Jesus to the world to be our Savior. Write in your journal and tell how baby Jesus came to earth.

What are your favorite Christmas books about Jesus? If you wrote a book about baby Jesus, what would its cover look like?

I have loved you with an everlasting love.

(Jeremiah 31:3 NIV)

God's love in Jesus lasts forever. Color this valentine for Jesus. Thank Him for living and dying for you.

Tell the world what Christmas is about! Decorate this sign to tell everyone who drives by about Jesus.

Do you see banners about Jesus in your church at Christmas time? Design this banner to welcome baby Jesus.

An angel of the Lord appeared to [the shepherds] and the glory of the Lord shone around them, and they were terrified. But the angel said to them, "Do not be afraid. I bring you good news."

(Luke 2:9–10 NIV)

An angel told the shepherds the good news about Jesus' birth. Draw one of God's angels in the sky.

Christmas cards are a good way to tell our friends about Jesus. Design a Christmas card to give to your best friend—one that will tell of Jesus' love.

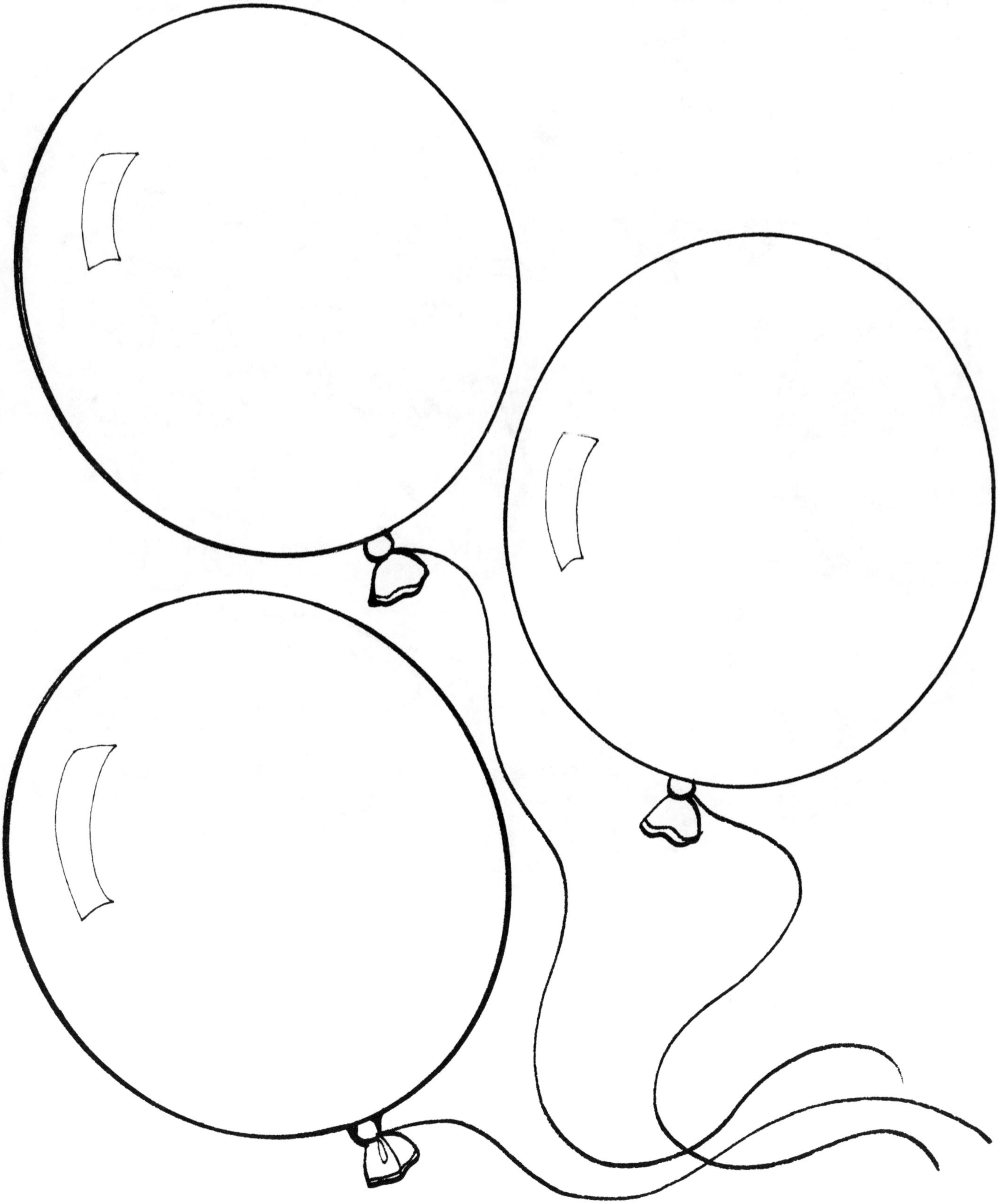

People like to decorate with balloons at a birthday party. Write messages and draw pictures on these balloons that will tell people about Jesus' birthday.

Joseph, Jesus' earthly father, was a carpenter. Circle and color the things he might have made for Jesus on His first birthday.

In Bible times, women sewed all the family's clothing. Find and color the clothes that Mary might have made for Jesus.

This lamb heard the angels sing and ran with his shepherds to find baby Jesus in the manger. What would the lamb say about his exciting night? Write his story in the speech balloon.

A Christmas tree points to heaven and reminds us of Jesus. It is "ever green" and reminds us that we will live forever with Jesus. Decorate these ornaments to tell people this good news.

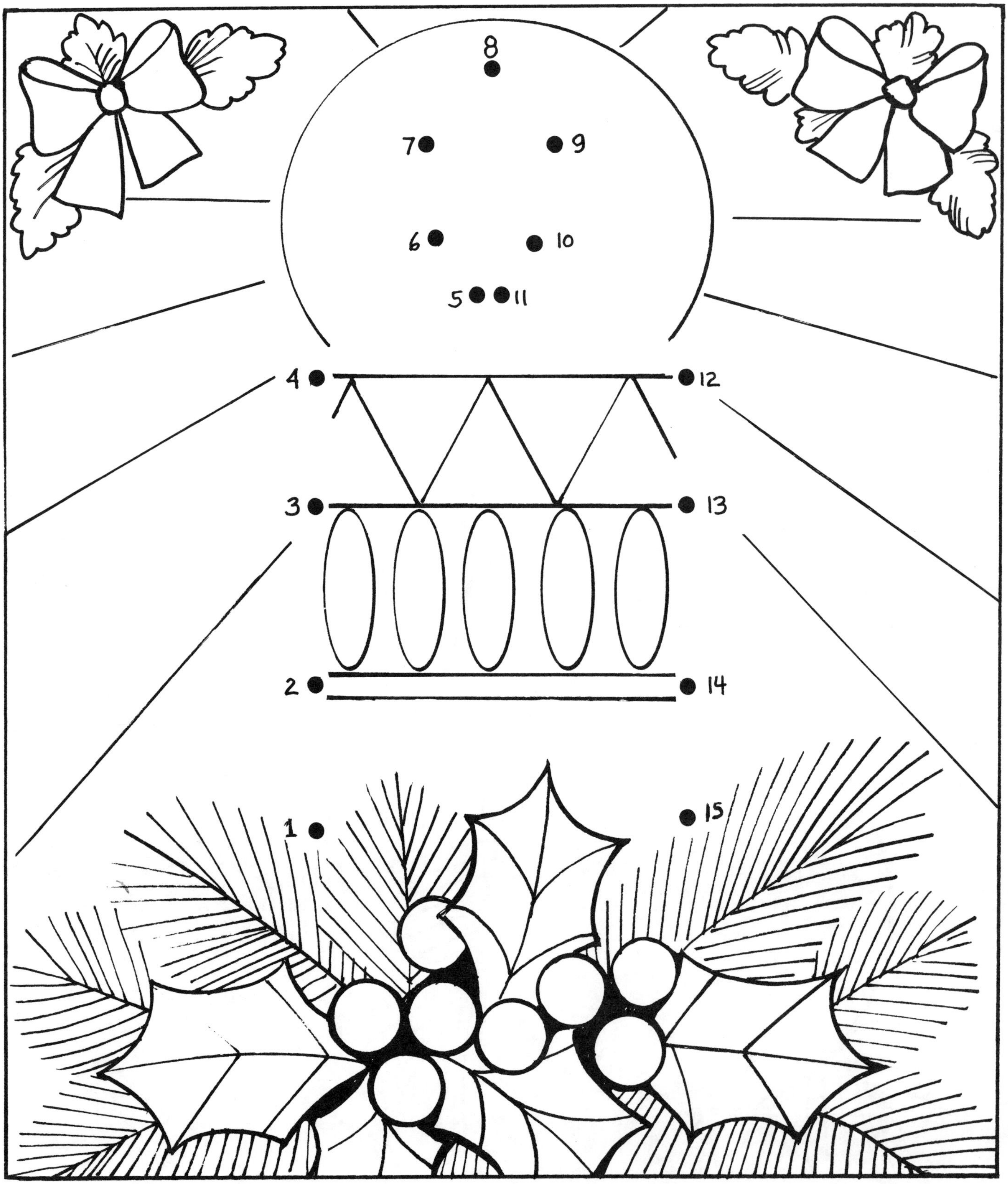

Jesus is the Light of the world. He forgives the darkness of our sins and lights the way to heaven. Connect the dots and decorate this Christmas candle.